Welcome to ALADDIN QUIX!

If you are looking for fast, fun-to-read stories with colorful characters, lots of kid-friendly humor, easy-to-follow action, entertaining story lines, and lively illustrations, then **ALADDIN QUIX** is for you!

But wait, there's more!

If you're also looking for stories with tables of contents; word lists; about-the-book questions; 64, 80, or 96 pages; short chapters; short paragraphs; and large fonts, then **ALADDIN QUIX** is *definitely* for you!

ALADDIN QUIX: The next step between ready to reads and longer, more challenging chapter books, for readers five to eight years old.

Read more ALADDIN QUIX books!

Our Principal Is a Frog!
by Stephanie Calmenson

Royal Sweets 1: A Royal Rescue
by Helen Perelman

Royal Sweets 2: Sugar Secrets
by Helen Perelman

A Miss Mallard Mystery: Dig to Disaster
by Robert Quackenbush

A Miss Mallard Mystery: Texas Trail to Calamity
by Robert Quackenbush

A Miss Mallard Mystery: Express Train to Trouble
by Robert Quackenbush

A Miss Mallard Mystery: Stairway to Doom
by Robert Quackenbush

Our Principal Is a Wolf!

BY **Stephanie Calmenson**

ILLUSTRATED BY
Aaron Blecha

ALADDIN QUIX

New York London Toronto Sydney New Delhi

To you, my reader

—S. C.

ALADDIN QUIX
Simon & Schuster Children's Publishing Division
1230 Avenue of the Americas, New York, New York 10020
First Aladdin QUIX hardcover edition September 2018
Text copyright © 2018 by Stephanie Calmenson
Illustrations copyright © 2018 by Aaron Blecha
Also available in an Aladdin QUIX paperback edition.
All rights reserved, including the right of reproduction in whole or in part in any form.
ALADDIN and the related marks and colophon
are trademarks of Simon & Schuster, Inc.
For information about special discounts for
bulk purchases, please contact Simon & Schuster Special Sales
at 1-866-506-1949 or business@simonandschuster.com.
The Simon & Schuster Speakers Bureau can bring authors to your live event. For more information or to book an event contact the Simon & Schuster Speakers Bureau at 1-866-248-3049 or visit our website at www.simonspeakers.com.
Jacket designed by Karin Paprocki
Interior designed by Heather Palisi and Karin Paprocki
The illustrations for this book were rendered digitally.
The text of this book was set in Archer Medium.
Manufactured in the United States of America 0818 FFG
2 4 6 8 10 9 7 5 3 1
Library of Congress Control Number 2018949110
ISBN 978-1-4814-6669-1 (hc)
ISBN 978-1-4814-6668-4 (pbk)
ISBN 978-1-4814-6670-7 (eBook)

Cast of Characters

Ms. Marilyn Moore: Assistant principal

Mr. Barnaby Bundy: Principal

Nancy Wong: Hopes to be a zoologist

Roger Patel: Top student and class leader

Max Berger: Excellent artist

Mrs. Gwen Feeny: Third-grade teacher

Alice Wright: Very helpful kindergarten student

Hector Gonzalez: Loves making his friends laugh

Ms. Ellie Tilly: Kindergarten teacher

Marty Q. Marvel: Bumbling magician

Ms. Karen Cole: School nurse

Wolfy (the wolf): Promises to be an excellent student

Contents

1

Luckiest Principal

A few days before spring break, **Ms. Moore** held a secret school assembly while **Mr. Bundy** was away at a meeting. She had a special plan she wanted to share with the students and teachers.

"Next month is Mr. Bundy's fifth anniversary as principal of PS 88. I would like to get him a gift from us all to show our appreciation."

Everyone loved the idea.

"Mr. Bundy loves clothes," said Nancy. **"Let's get him a tie!"**

"He's got so many ties already," said **Roger**.

"How about a new bell for his bike?" said **Max**.

Mr. Bundy rode his bicycle to school, rain or shine.

"A new bike bell would be good," said **Mrs. Feeny**. "But I think he just got one."

Thinking about Mr. Bundy's bike gave Ms. Moore an idea.

"Yesterday, he got caught in the rain riding home from school," she said. "Why don't we get him a rain poncho to keep in his briefcase?"

The idea was a big hit.

Knowing Mr. Bundy was a sharp dresser, Ms. Moore said, "I'll pick up a shiny red poncho to match his shiny red bike."

At the end of the week, Mr. Bundy held his own assembly to wish everyone a good spring break. It was the perfect time to give him his gift.

Alice, a kindergarten student, sang a song she wrote for the occasion.

"Happy anniversary,
Mr. Bundy!
Thank you for all you do.
You take the best care
of our school.
So we want to take
good care of you!"

"Thank you, everyone!" said Mr. Bundy. "I am the luckiest principal in town!"

He wiped the happy tears from his eyes with his crisply ironed handkerchief. Then he put on his new poncho and got a big round of applause.

Spring break turned out to be chilly and rainy, so Mr. Bundy got to wear his new poncho a lot. Riding around town, he waved to his students, who were glad to  see him enjoying his gift. **"Lookin' good, Mr. B!"** **they called.**

2

Greetings!

On the last night of vacation, Mr. Bundy's phone rang. It was Ms. Moore. She sounded awful.

"I have a tewwibul code," she moaned. "I'm sowwy, but I haf to miff school tomowwow."

Mr. Bundy exclaimed, "**Poor Ms. Moore!** We'll miss you, but you must stay home and rest."

Mr. Bundy wanted to do something to help his good friend and assistant principal feel better. So he got to work making a hearty soup for Ms. Moore.

The next morning, Mr. Bundy got up extra early to leave plenty of time to deliver the soup before going to school.

Since it was drizzling lightly when he started out on his bicycle, he put on his beloved red poncho and pedaled toward Ms. Moore's house. Her house was outside the town, a little way into the woods.

As he pedaled along, Mr. Bundy sang new words to the tune of Alice's song.

"I'm on my way,
Ms. Moore.
I thank you for all you do.
I'm very sorry you're sick.
My soup will be
good for you!"

Mr. Bundy was happily sing-ing and pedaling, and pedaling and singing, when he saw a hairy, bearded man right in the middle of his path.

"Greetings!" said the man in a **raspy**, barky voice. "Who are

you, and where are you off to in such a hurry?"

"I'm Mr. Bundy, the principal of PS 88, and I'm delivering soup to my assistant principal, Ms. Moore. She's sick with a terrible cold," said Mr. Bundy.

"How nice of you," said the hairy, bearded man.

This was just the kind of opportunity the hairy, bearded man had been waiting for. He thought quickly.

"Soup is a fine thing to bring," he said. "But take a look around you. With all the rain we've been having, the flowers have grown very beautiful. Wouldn't you like to give your assistant principal a pretty **bouquet**?"

Mr. Bundy looked at the flowers.

"That's an excellent idea!" he said.

"Tell me, where does Ms. Moore live?" asked the hairy, bearded man. "I'm new in town. She and I might be neighbors."

Mr. Bundy described her house and location exactly.

"Ah, yes, I've seen it, and it's lovely. I'm glad we had this little talk," said the hairy, bearded man.

Mr. Bundy couldn't help noticing the man's long nose and big teeth. In fact, he reminded Mr.

Bundy of his great-uncle Jasper. But there was *something* different about him. He just couldn't put his finger on what it was.

"Take your time picking your bouquet," said the man. "I think you'll find that the most beautiful flowers are a little deeper in the woods."

The hairy, bearded man wanted to give himself as much time as possible to carry out his plan.

"Thank you," said Mr. Bundy. "A bouquet to go with

my soup will be perfect."

Mr. Bundy leaned his bike against a tree and started into the woods to gather the most beautiful flowers he could find.

Meanwhile, the hairy, bearded man raced to Ms. Moore's house. Mr. Bundy had been right about him. There *was* something different. The hairy, bearded man wasn't a man at all. He was a hungry young wolf in **disguise**!

3

Yum, Yum, Yum!

It was good of Mr. Bundy to give me such exact directions, thought the wolf as he set off for Ms. Moore's house.

It didn't take him long to get there.

Knock, knock, knock!
Knock, knock, knock!

"Who is it?" called Ms. Moore weakly from her sickbed.

"It's me! Mr. Bundy! I brought you some goodies!" answered the wolf.

"Oh, how nice," said Ms. Moore. "I'm too **weary** to come to the door. But there's a key in the flowerpot. Let yourself in."

Those words were music to the wolf's ears. He found the key, and before Ms. Moore knew what was happening, the hungry wolf ate her up in one big bite.

"**Yum, yum, yum!**

That assistant principal was a very tasty treat," the wolf said to himself. "I bet the principal will be even tastier!"

The wolf quickly put on one of Ms. Moore's nightgowns and the nightcap he found under her pillow.

He hopped into her bed, pulled up the covers, and waited for his next delicious course.

A short time later, Mr. Bundy arrived at Ms. Moore's house with the soup and a huge bouquet.

He was surprised to see the door
wide open.

*Maybe she's feeling better and
has gone out for a stroll,* he thought.
"Ms. Moore! Ms. Moore!"
he called.

"I'm in here," said a raspy voice.

My poor friend. She sounds even worse than last night, thought Mr. Bundy.

He took off his poncho, hung it on a chair, then went to her room. He saw Ms. Moore in bed, with the covers pulled up almost to her nightcap. He thought her illness was making her look *very* strange.

"My, what big eyes you have," said Mr. Bundy.

"The better to see you with," said the raspy voice.

"What big ears you have," said Mr. Bundy.

"The better to hear you with," said the raspy voice.

The bedcover slipped down.

"My, what big teeth you have," said Mr. Bundy.

"The better to EAT you with!" said the raspy voice.

Then the wolf popped out of bed and gobbled up Mr. Bundy in one big bite, soup, flowers and all.

"Yum, yum, yum!" said the wolf, smacking his lips. "That was a very tasty principal indeed."

4

Who's for Dessert?

Hmm, thought the wolf. *If the assistant principal and the principal were so tasty, I can only imagine how delicious their students will be.*

He quickly spit out Mr. Bundy's

clothes and put them on. (They had tasted terrible, anyway.) Then he grabbed Mr. Bundy's red poncho and threw it over his head.

For a final touch, he went to Ms. Moore's bathroom and used a few dabs of her hair gel to slick his fur down neatly.

"How handsome I look!" he said, winking at himself in the mirror.

The wolf raced out of Ms. Moore's house and jumped onto Mr. Bundy's bicycle.

He pedaled off as fast as he could go with the red poncho flying behind him in the breeze.

He followed the road signs leading to PS 88, arriving just in time to greet the students.

Here comes my dessert, thought the wolf, seeing the first children arrive.

"Good morning, Mr. Bundy!" said **Hector**. "That's a great beard you grew over spring break."

"It sure is," said Roger. **"Lookin' good, Mr. B!"**

"Thank you, boys," replied the wolf, coughing a little. "You'll have to excuse my raspy voice today. I'm a little under the weather."

Once the bell rang, the wolf followed the students and teachers inside the school. He decided to visit the classrooms one by one.

I'll start with the little students first. They'll be excellent taste-bud teasers, he thought with a chuckle.

The wolf knocked on **Ms. Tilly**'s kindergarten door.

He walked in with a big drooly smile.

"Hi, Mr. Bundy!" said Alice. "I like your new beard. Would

you please read us a story?"

Little Alice was so charming that the wolf had second thoughts about making her his first bite of dessert.

"Of course I'll read a story," he replied.

He wanted to prove to himself that he was not completely hard-hearted.

I'll let her enjoy the story, and then I'll gobble her up, he thought.

"Will you read this one?" asked Alice.

She handed him a copy of *Little Red Riding Hood.*

"A fine choice," **snickered** the wolf. And he began to read.

"'Once upon a time, there was a little girl whose grandmother

gave her a beautiful red cape. The girl loved it so much, she wore it all the time. So everyone called her Little Red Riding Hood.'"

Just then, there was another knock at the kindergarten door. **Knock, knock!**

It was Roger with a note from his teacher for Ms. Tilly. Roger didn't want to interrupt when he saw the class listening to a story, so he sat down to listen too.

When it came to the part where the grandmother was about to

be eaten, Roger saw Mr. Bundy's eyes growing bigger. He saw his mouth watering.

He saw Mr. Bundy looking at the kindergarten students as though they were huge scoops of ice cream with hot fudge and whipped cream on top.

Roger started to worry because Mr. Bundy didn't seem quite like himself. In fact, he seemed a little wolfish.

First there was his raspy voice. Of course, Mr. Bundy had said he was under the weather.

There was also his new beard. But Mr. B probably grew it to mark his anniversary at PS 88 with a new look.

I'm being silly, thought Roger.

Then he froze. He thought he saw something furry poking out from the back of Mr. Bundy's suit.

I sure have a good imagination, Roger thought. *Just because I'm listening to a story with a wolf in it, I think I'm seeing—*

Suddenly, the furry thing flicked back and forth. It wasn't Roger's imagination.

It was a tail!

5

Wolfy's Promise

"I'll ... I'll be right back!" croaked Roger, leaping up and racing out of the room.

There wasn't a moment to waste. Roger had to do something, and fast! He knew Ms. Moore was out sick, so he couldn't go to her for help. He had no time to gather up his friends.

And he didn't think any of the teachers would believe him if he tried to explain that Mr. Bundy wasn't Mr. Bundy but a wolf!

Roger ran down the hall to Mr. Bundy's office. The last time he was there, he had seen a magician's business card on the desk.

It was a long shot. A long, long, long shot. But Roger had to try. He found the card and made the call.

Thank goodness, the magician answered. Roger explained the problem as quickly as he could.

In the blink of an eye, a man wearing a tall black hat and a magician's cape tripped into Mr. Bundy's office in a cloud of green smoke.

"Whoops! **Marty Q. Marvel**, here, fresh from a six-month advanced magician's course in sunny Aloha Kona, Hawaii. Allow me to amaze, **confound** and **astound** you!" he said.

"Follow me!" said Roger.

"We've got to hurry!"

They raced to Ms. Tilly's room. Roger was afraid to go in, fearing he was too late. But he was amazed when he opened the door. The wolf was weaving in and out of the circle of kindergarteners, singing:

"Bluebird, bluebird,
through my window.
Bluebird, bluebird,
through my window!"

"Come join us!" he said cheerily. **"I've never had so much fun!"**

Of course, the kindergarteners thought they were dancing and singing with their beloved principal, Mr. Bundy.

Thanks to Roger, Marty Q. Marvel knew the real story and wasn't about to fall for any big-bad-wolf tricks.

Marty quickly waved his magic wand, chanting,

And a-one!

"And a-one, and a-two,
and a-one, two, three.
Mean old wolf,
you're history!"

Nothing happened. He waved his wand again. Still nothing.

"I knew I shouldn't have skipped my wolf-disappearing class," moaned Marty.

The wolf looked at him with fear and hurt in his eyes. In his short time in the kindergarten class, he had grown to love the youngest students at PS 88.

But his secret was out. Ms. Tilly gathered her frightened students close by her side.

What will I do? the wolf thought.

Now that they know I'm a wolf and not Mr. Bundy, I'll have to eat everyone in the room.

Alice didn't like the hungry gleam she saw in the wolf's eyes. She remembered how happy and friendly he was when he was dancing and singing. That gave her an idea.

She ran to the wolf, grabbed his paw and started to sing the Hokey Pokey song.

"You put your right paw in!

*You take your
right paw out!
You put your
right paw in,
then you shake it
all about!"*

The wolf started swaying to the tune and joined Alice doing the Hokey Pokey.

Meanwhile, Roger was thinking, *If this isn't Mr. Bundy, where is Mr. Bundy? And is Ms. Moore really out sick, or is she . . .*

Oh no! Roger thought and started singing as fast as he could.

"You spin to your left!
You spin to your right!
Spin round and round
with all of your might!"

The wolf spun round and round. Round and round, faster and faster. He was having so much fun, he threw back his head, opened his mouth, and yelled, **"Wheeee!"**

Out flew Ms. Moore! Out flew Mr. Bundy!

WHEEE!

Everyone gasped as the tired, dizzy wolf fell to the floor, panting. Then he started to cry.

"I'm sorry," he sobbed. "Yes, it's true that I'm a wolf who ate people to survive. But that was before I met all of you. Please give me a chance to start over. Please let me be a student at PS 88. I love this school, and

I promise to be good!"

The wolf cried so hard that the school nurse, **Ms. Cole**, was called in to take care of him.

"We forgive you," said Ms. Moore, who, surprisingly, was feeling quite a bit better.

"Roger and Alice, thank you for rescuing us," said Mr. Bundy. "Marty Q. Marvel, thank you for trying."

Mr. Bundy turned and spoke to the **bedraggled** wolf.

"We will give you a chance

to join us here at PS 88. But you must follow every rule," he warned.

"I will! I will!" said the wolf, perking up.

"And no more gobbling up anyone," added Mr. Bundy.

"I won't! I won't!" replied the wolf.

"And you must give me back my red poncho," said Mr. Bundy.

"Aww, do I have to?" said the wolf. "I really like it a lot. And I look so handsome in it."

"Yes, you have to," said the principal, rolling his eyes.

A few weeks later, Mr. Bundy visited Ms. Tilly's kindergarten to ask how the wolf was doing.

"**Wolfy**'s quite an **exceptional** student," replied Ms. Tilly. "Every morning, he recites his own **pledge** of **allegiance**."

"**Really?**" said Mr. Bundy. "I'd like to hear it."

Wolfy was proud to be asked. He stood up, put his hand over his heart and began.

"I pledge allegiance
to PS 88,
where the principals,
teachers and
kids are all great.
I promise to follow
each and every rule.
I'll be the best student
at this excellent school.
I'll work hard learning
to read and to write.
I won't eat any
more people.
No, I won't take a bite."

"Bravo!" cheered Mr. Bundy. He clapped as Wolfy took a bow.

Walking back to his office, Mr. Bundy smiled, thinking about his years at PS 88.

Happy anniversary to me, he thought. *I am surely the luckiest principal in town!*

Word List

allegiance (a•LEE•jents):
Loyalty or faithfulness

astound (a•STOWND): To
surprise greatly

bedraggled (be•DRAG•guld):
Dirty or messy

bouquet (boo•KAY): A bunch
of flowers arranged in a
pleasing way

confound (con•FOUND):
To surprise and amaze

disguise (diss•GIZE):
Something used to change
how one looks in order to not
be recognized

exceptional (ek•SEP•shun•ul):
Unusually good

pledge (PLEJ): A very serious
promise

raspy (RA•spee): Rough- and
harsh-sounding

snickered (SNI•kerd):
Giggled in a covered-up
smarty-pants way

weary (WEE•ree): Very tired

Questions

1. What gift would you give to your principal?
2. Have you ever been surprised to learn that a person is different from what you expected?
3. Do you think a person can change? How about a wolf?
4. Would you like Wolfy to be in your class?